For
SYLVIE AND
WAYLAND

Little friends, far away.

Stan Stinky
vs the
SEWER PiRATes

Written and illustrated by

HANNAH SHAW

■SCHOLASTIC

First published in the UK in 2014 by Scholastic Children's Books
An imprint of Scholastic Ltd
Euston House, 24 Eversholt Street
London, NW1 1DB, UK
Registered office: Westfield Road, Southam, Warwickshire, CV47 0RA
SCHOLASTIC and associated logos are trademarks and/or registered
trademarks of Scholastic Inc.

ISBN 978 14071 3641 7

A CIP catalogue record for this book is available from the
British Library.

Printed and bound by CPI Group (UK) Ltd., Croydon, CR0 4YY
Papers used by Scholastic Children's Books are made from
wood grown in sustainable forests.

1 3 5 7 9 10 8 6 4 2

This is a work of fiction. Names, characters, places, incidents
and dialogues are products of the author's imagination or are used
fictitiously. Any resemblance to actual people, living or dead, events
or locales is entirely coincidental.

www.scholastic.co.uk

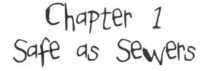

Chapter 1
Safe as Sewers

"Stan! Yoohoo!"

Stan was waiting at the bus stop when he saw Olive Copperpipe running towards him, legs and arms flailing madly. Olive was new to his class; she'd only just joined Rat School after the summer holidays and had already caused a bit of a stir because she was incredibly talkative and

LOUD!

"YOU DROPPED THIS!" Olive handed Stan his gnawed pencil and loo-roll notebook.

"Thanks, Olive!" Stan was relieved – his notebook was super important because it was where he wrote all his thoughts and ideas. It was especially important at the moment because of the new TOP-SECRET project he was working on.

SO, STAN, YOU'RE TRYING TO BE A DETECTIVE?!

Olive yelled.

"'Hey!" frowned Stan. "Keep your voice down – I want to keep it a secret!"

Olive didn't take any notice. "Are you really a detective? How many crimes have you solved? Oooh, is that what you're going to do for your CLASS TALK? Mrs Scratchy says everyone has to speak for ten whole minutes on their subject. But you'll probably have so much to say you'll need to speak for longer!"

"Err. . ." Stan didn't want to admit that he'd never solved a single crime.

"Well, I'm going to do my Class Talk on GUARD ANTS. My guard ant Antony—"

Olive was cut off by the clang of the old baked-bean-can bus arriving. Choking smoke from its engine filled the pipe.

"Oh, do you live at drain level then?" Olive asked as Stan backed away from her on to the bus. "I live in Brownwater. I have to catch a SILLY OLD BOAT FERRY to school and home again. . ."

Olive was still talking as the bus pulled away. Stan watched her disappear out of the grimy back window. He chuckled to himself and rubbed his ears. Olive could talk the hind legs off a grasshopper.

As the bus bumped along, the seats tainted by the whiff of mouldy beans, Stan glanced around at his fellow passengers. They were all grown up and BORING.

Stan wished he could live in the village of Brownwater or the main town of Slime-on-the-Sewer and take the boat ferry to school with all the other rats in his class. His home was at drain level, which was the dullest part of the sewer – Stan had hardly anyone his own age to play with.

Plus, he lived so far away from the sewer rivers that, before last summer, he'd never learnt to swim (which was unheard of for a sewer rat). It was only thanks to an adventure with his crazy uncle Captain Ratts and his cockroach sidekick Roachy on their boat, The Old Noodle, that Stan had managed to teach himself. He'd also learnt to surf and encountered a real live human! Captain Ratts had named Stan his Chief Adventurer and they'd made headline news for saving the sewers from an underwear disaster. Captain Ratts had been given two gold taps from the Mayor as a reward. It was the best summer Stan had ever had and since then he'd been trying to find something equally exciting to do.

But excitement was quite hard to come by at drain level. The most exciting thing that had happened recently was a human emptying a can of cola into their lounge, narrowly missing his mum. Stan had spent an entire evening helping her remove the sticky mess from the floor. That was about as action-packed as it got. Instead Stan READ about adventure. He waited eagerly each week for his detective comic to be delivered. It starred his favourite cartoon character, INSPECTOR SPY-DER, an impossibly cool crime-solving spider whose ability to hang from the ceiling and weave invisible webs to spy on suspects made him very good at his job.

Wouldn't it be great to be like SPY-DER?
thought Stan. He smiled to himself as he
opened his notebook, where he'd recently
glued a drawing of his hero. Olive had
guessed right; he was planning to surprise
everyone and speak about being a detective
for his Class Talk. He looked at what he'd
done so far. . .

BEING A DETECTIVE, BY STAN STINKY

Things I still need to become a proper detective:

- Detective equipment:

Camera

magnifying glass

binoculars

undercover disguises
(e.g. dark glasses)

- Advice from a real detective like Chief Inspector Dung at the police station
- A crime to solve

Stan sighed. The last one of these was the trickiest. Where in the sewers was he going to find a genuine crime?

Arriving home, Stan opened his rusty tin front door, which gave its usual squeak, and noticed with a happy sniff that grub sausages were sizzling in the pan. His mum was back from work early.

"Hi, Stan! Did you have a nice day? Excellent news in the paper today. The sewers are officially CRIME FREE!"

NOOOOO! Stan's face dropped. "Crime free? No crime at all, anywhere? Let me see!" He grabbed the paper from his mum.

"Pah!" Stan said. "And to think I was going to call Inspector Dung for my project."

But his mum wasn't listening. She was reading a copy of *Smello!* magazine and cooing over the glossy photographs of celebrities. Stan read over her shoulder.

SMELLO! MAGAZINE

Reformed criminal Max Weavels reveals the secret to goodness and throws charity gala.

"IT'S GOOD TO BE GOOD"

Max Weavels has come a long way from his days as a master con artist and thief. Now he likes nothing better than being good. All the money raised from his fancy dress business, Max's Disguises, will go into his new project, a home for Abandoned Pigeons and Other Outcast Pests (A POOP).

"I want to help others see that being good is a good thing to be, so I hired some ex-prisoners to work in the home," Max declared.

And, finally, to celebrate the sewers being declared crime free, Max has given Inspector Dung a ticket for a round-the-world trip, starting at the Dung Pyramids of Ancient Egypt.

When asked about his generosity, Max said modestly, "It's good to be good."

Stan threw down the magazine in disgust. "Humph. Even the criminals have turned boring!"

After grub sausages and mashed potato peelings, Stan's mum remembered that she'd forgotten to give Stan his post. It was a letter from Uncle Ratts. Stan had written to him ages ago about his detective project and had been waiting eagerly for a reply.

Stan Stinky

AIR MAIL

The Old Noodle
Slime-on-
the-Sewer

THE HARBOUR'S
NO.1 GREASY
RAT TAIL DINER

Dear Stan,
Excellent to hear from you!
Roachy and I have been moored
up in Slime-on-the-Sewer
harbour eating lots of fried
breakfasts and catching up with
old friends. I haven't seen much
of the Mayor recently because

he's been hanging out with his new friend Mr "Goody-Two-Shoes" Max Weavels. He has really been getting on my nerves with his do-gooder nonsense. "It's gooood to be goood!" Zzzz! I'm very interested to hear that you're keen to be a detective. If you need any help solving a crime, we're ready to take on the baddies with you. (Just as long as it's after breakfast.) As you know, adventure is our game and, er . . . so on and so forth.

Yours greasily,

Captain Ratts   Roachy

Too bad there are no crimes to solve, thought Stan as he brushed his teeth. *What am I going to do my Class Talk on now?*

"Mum," asked Stan when she came to kiss him goodnight, "can we get a guard ant? Olive Copperpipe has one and she's going to bring him in for her Class Talk."

"Sorry, Stan. I'm allergic to ant hairs."

Stan sighed. *Then again*, he thought as he drifted off to sleep, *what use is a guard ant when there is nothing to guard against?*

Chapter 2
New Tricks

"Quiet, everyone! Back in your seats!" Mrs Scratchy shouted over the din of squeaking rats.

Olive Copperpipe was standing at the front of the classroom. She was holding a tiny cushion made from sweet wrappers and upon it was perched the cutest ant Stan had ever seen. Its huge eyes glistened and its little sting wagged. The class were all very excited. Fiona Fleabag was making coo-cooing noises.

It doesn't look much like a guard ant, thought Stan. *It couldn't scare a gnat!* "THIS IS ANTONY," Olive boomed.

"His favourite food is jam sandwiches. . . He's learning to be good at guarding things. . . And he can do tricks too!"

"Oooh, make him do a trick!" said Fiona Fleabag.

Olive looked worried for a second but then turned towards Antony. She looked sternly at him. "Antony, sit!"

Antony just stared at her.

"I said SIT." Olive looked at him even more sternly.

Antony wagged his little sting . . . and lay down.

"Er, he gets a bit confused between lying down and sitting," Olive explained. "I'll show you his begging trick instead."

Holding a piece of jam sandwich,

she waved it in front of Antony's nose. "Antony, BEG!"

Antony took a look at the sandwich, leapt into the air and snatched it straight out of her paw, swallowing it in one gulp.

"He also gets a bit confused between beg and, er . . . jump!" Olive was blushing now. "But he's really good at guarding. Let me show you!" She fumbled in a bag and took out a large, very expensive-looking silver bottle top. She placed it on the floor.

"Now, Antony," she began. . .

"Well, well, well. What do we have here?"

came a voice from the doorway.

Well, well, well.

Stan looked round to see

a tall figure that looked strangely familiar.

Mrs Scratchy's face lit up with delight. "Mr Weavels! You're early! Come in, come in!"

Of course – Max Weavels! Stan remembered him now from his mum's copy of *Smello!* magazine. He was still dressed in a snappy suit and shiny shoes.

"Children, let me introduce you to Mr Max Weavels. He's come to talk to you all about his successful career and why it's good to be good."

"Delighted!" Max Weavels gave a smirky sort of smile and sat down. He smelled funny. *Too much Eau de Loo*

Cleaner, thought Stan.

"Now, don't mind me, dear," Max Weavels said to Olive. "I'd be fascinated to see your ant's trick."

Olive continued. "Where was I? Oh, yes, Antony was going to do his guarding trick." She pointed once more to the shiny bottle top. "This is from my dad's priceless bottle top collection. It's just one of a hundred and three bottle tops he's collected. Antony's main job is to guard the collection."

Stan noticed Max Weavels suddenly lean forward in an interested way.

Olive gave Antony a look of desperation.

"ANTONY, GUARD!"

Antony sniffed the bottle top in a bored

way. Then he fell asleep.

The whole class burst into laughter. Stan felt a bit sorry for poor Olive.

Max Weavels stood up and patted her on the head. "Well, that was VERY insightful. And I was sooo interested to hear all about your father's priceless bottle top collection." He bent down and admired the one in front of him. "What a beauty!"

Antony opened one eye.

"Sweet little ant," said Max. He reached to pat him and Antony nipped at his arm.

Maybe Antony doesn't like his aftershave either, Stan thought.

"I'm so sorry, Mr Weavels!" Mrs Scratchy gushed, hurrying Olive back to her seat with Antony in tow. "Would you like to speak to the class now?"

Max Weavels gave the class a big grin. "Well, well, my young ratlings. It's charming to be here today in your school. I am a very busy rat, but I always like to make time to meet my fans." He winked at Mrs Scratchy, who went pink. "I'm here to tell you my life story. You see, I used to be a bit of a bad rat. . . That's how I ended up in Rat-a-Traz."

Max Weavels paused for effect. Stan's classmates gasped.

Rat-a-Traz was a human pet shop and all rats knew that it was where you were sent if you'd been very, VERY bad.

"In Rat-a-Traz they keep you locked up in a cage, make you run constantly in an exercise wheel and feed you nothing but dried peas. Some of my cage-mates got sold to human children as pets! Has anyone ever seen a human child?"

Stan had, on his summer adventure, and he didn't wish to meet another.

Max Weavels went on. "They are like big, adult humans, but completely OUT OF CONTROL!"

He wiped his brow, as if still suffering from the trauma of it all.

"Believe me, I learned the error of my ways. Eventually I was released for good behaviour. Since becoming a free rat, I've worked hard and made an enormous fortune running my fancy dress shop, Max's Disguises. And I spend all my free time helping the needy. I've recently set up a home for Abandoned Pigeons and Other Outcast Pests on the waterfront, with the help of other former criminals. I'm now a MODEL CITIZEN. It's good to be GOOD!"

Max smiled and stroked his moustache. He seemed very pleased with himself. Stan decided he didn't like him one bit, and while the rest of the class asked Max for autographs and photos, he thought he'd practise being a detective by taking some notes.

Stan got out his notebook and started drawing.

Then he wrote:

Then the bell rang and Mrs Scratchy said, "Class dismissed! Thank you, Mr Weavels, for a WONDERFUL presentation. Stan, you're giving the next talk. I only hope yours will be as good."

Stan gulped. With no crime to investigate, his talk about being a detective was going to send everyone to sleep!

Chapter 3
Ant-knapped

The next day was Saturday and there was no school. While his mum was busy doing boring parent things, Stan lay on his bed and piled his comics up around him.

He was immersed in an old SPY-DER cartoon when the doorbell clanked urgently.

Come in!

he heard his mum say.

So lovely to
meet one of Stan's
school friends!

Stan sat up. Someone from school had come to see him? At HOME? Usually none of his friends came over to his drain since it was so far away from the main sewer.

He hurried downstairs, where he found none other than Olive Copperpipe sitting at the kitchen table. She looked miserable, and the strangest thing was, she wasn't saying a word.

"Are you sure you're all right, dear?" his mum asked as she boiled the kettle for a cup of hot mouldy chocolate. "Terrible news, isn't it, about the burglaries? Especially after we were all told how safe we are now. I can't believe there are pirates in the sewers!"

Burglaries?! thought Stan. *PIRATES??*

"Here Stan is now," his mum said. "Well, I've got to pop out to the shops . . . hope I don't meet any pirates!" She laughed, but Stan noticed Olive didn't smile back. In fact, she looked as if she was about to cry.

As soon as Stan's mum left the room, Olive burst into tears. "Stan, you're a detective – you HAVE to HELP ME!!!" She pointed frantically at a copy of the *Daily Slime*.

The Daily Slim

2 RAT

BURGLARIES IN BROWNWATER
PIRATES
MAIN SUSPECTS

The residents of Brownwater had a shocking awakening this morning. During the night, burglars, thought to be PIRATES, broke into pipes in the sleepy village, stealing more than twenty sacks' worth of goods. Fred Copperpipe's cherished bottle top collection and Cheryl Fleabag's teaspoon were stolen, among other valuables such as expensive garden ornaments. Items were also taken from the local museum, the Museum of Shiny Things Accidentally Washed Down Human Plugholes.

SHINY THING

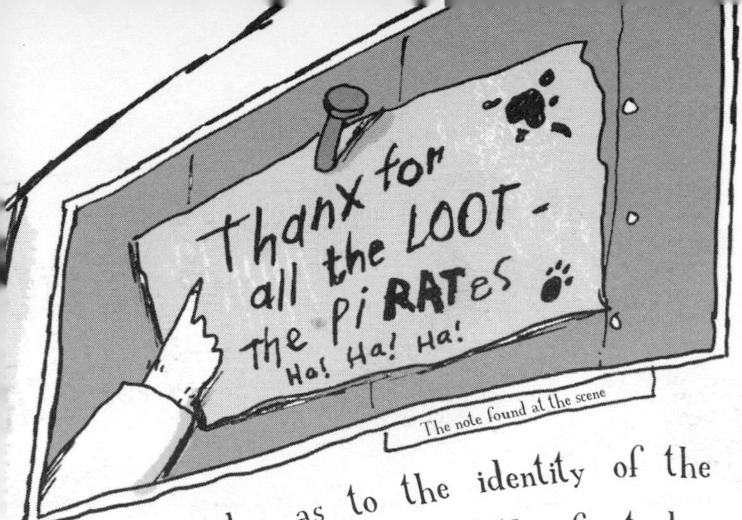
Thanx for
all the LOOT -
the piRATes
Ha! Ha! Ha!
The note found at the scene

The only clue as to the identity of the suspects is a note pinned to the front door of the museum.

Inspector Dung has returned home from his holiday today to start the investigation.

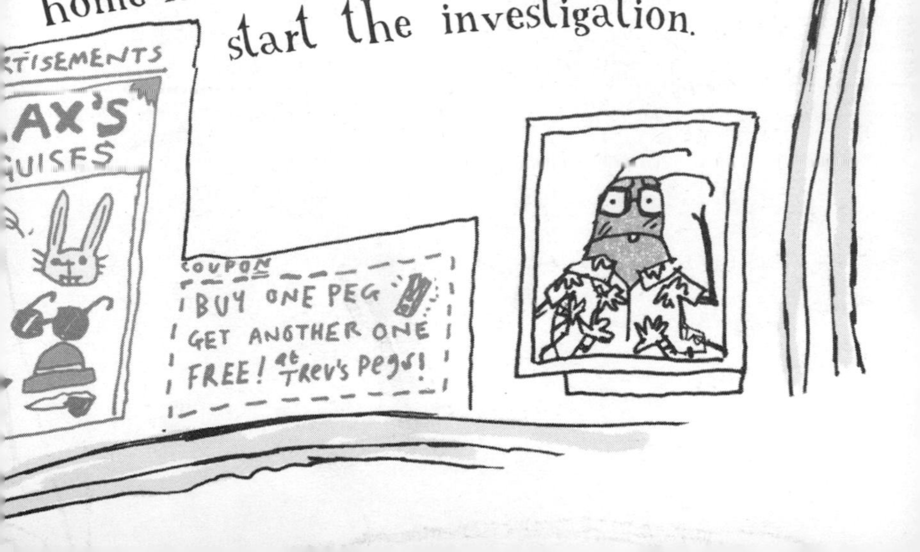
COUPON
BUY ONE PEG
GET ANOTHER ONE
FREE! at TREV's pegs!

Looks like the sewers aren't a hundred per cent crime free after all, thought Stan.

Not only have all of my dad's bottle tops gone . . . but so has ANTONY! He's been ant-knapped!

You've GOT to help me!

Stan stared at Olive. He felt sorry for her and all the residents who'd had their valuables stolen. But he was also excited. Finally, here was a crime to investigate!

"Please help me, Stan!" Olive pleaded. "You can use all your special detective knowledge to find Antony!" She handed Stan an envelope. "I even collected a clue for you."

OK, OK! I'll help you. But first, slow down and tell me everything.

And Stan fetched his detective notebook to begin the investigation.

INVESTIGATION:
The Case of the Missing Guard Ant

Name of victim: Antony

Owner: Olive Copperpipe

Missing from: No. 89

Brownwater View, Brownwater

Also missing from No 89
Brownwater View: 103 rare
bottle tops belonging to Mr Fred
Copperpipe

Witness statement from Olive Copperpipe:
"I put Antony to bed as normal. At midnight

I heard him barking but he always barks in his sleep so I didn't think anything of it. When I woke up, Antony and the bottle tops were gone! Then my dad said that Antony was a useless guard ant and he didn't know why we'd got him, and I got cross and stormed off."

Plan of Crime Scene:

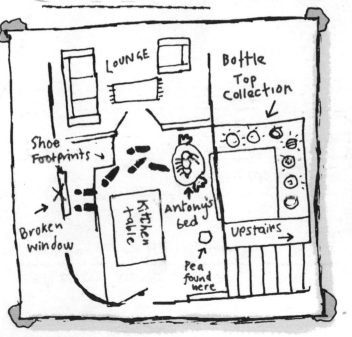

Clue: Pirate's note
Thanx for all the LOOT - the PiRATes
Ha! Ha! Ha!
The note found at the scene
Other Clue: Old Pea

"YUCK!" said Stan as he opened Olive's clue. "What's this? An old pea! Where did it come from?"

"I found it," said Olive proudly. "It was on the floor where Antony sleeps."

Stan looked closely at the pea. It looked a bit like pet-shop food. But there were no pet shops in the sewers. How strange. . . He thought carefully for a moment. "Olive, this is a VERY IMPORTANT clue," he said. "I think it's crucial you assist me with this investigation."

Chapter 4
Panic and Pigeons

"If they're pirates they must have a boat," Olive said anxiously. "That means they could have taken Antony anywhere."

They were studying the map of the sewers on Stan's bedroom wall.

"Let's go and talk to my uncle, Captain Ratts – he knows every boat on the River Gunk," Stan suggested.

WOWSER!
SPY·DER

Olive agreed and together they set off for
Slime-on-the-Sewer.

When the bus eventually dropped them
off at the harbour, Stan expected to see the

familiar rickety Old Noodle straight away. But although the pongy River Gunk was full of boats bobbing up and down, The Old Noodle was nowhere to be seen. Stan walked up and down the pipes and jetties and finally found the plastic-bottle dinghy that was usually attached to The Old Noodle, but the boat itself was gone.

"That's strange," Stan said. "If Captain Ratts has gone on an adventure,

I'd have thought he would at least tell me first. After all, I am his Chief Adventurer!"

"Well, this is a bad start," Olive said, looking upset. "How are we going to find Antony now?"

"Maybe the Mayor will be able to help," Stan suggested. "He and my uncle are best friends." He thought back to the letter his uncle had sent. Even if they weren't hanging out so much any more, the Mayor would certainly know if Captain Ratts had left town. "Let's go and ask him."

The Mayor lived in the Town Hall Pipe, the most beautiful and lavish pipe in the whole of the sewers. It was crammed with the Ancient Sewer Council's precious relics, as well as being furnished with grand statues, paintings and a gold bottle-top ceiling.

When Stan and Olive reached the Town Hall Pipe

they saw a huge crowd gathered outside.
Bugs and rats jostled to get
closer to the front.
The Mayor was
standing on the top
step, wiping his
brow. Next to him
was Inspector Dung.
Stan recognized
the reporter from
the *Daily Slime*
scribbling away
in a notebook.

The Mayor waved his paws in the air.

SILENCE PLEASE!

"I know many of you are worried about the burglaries in Brownwater, but we are appealing for CALM. Now, Inspector Dung here has an important announcement to make."

Inspector Dung picked up the megaphone.

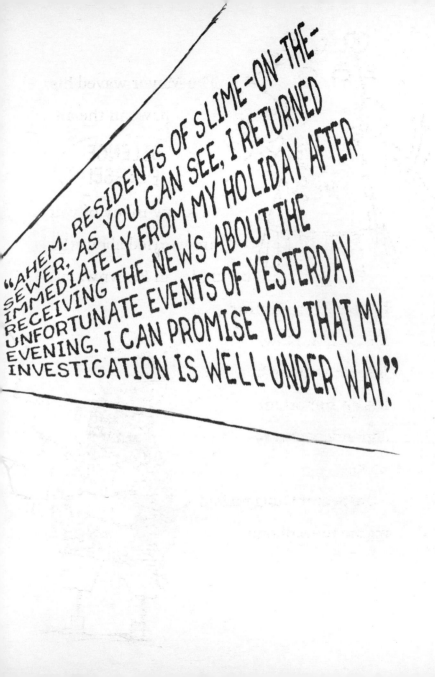

A nervous murmur bubbled from the crowd.

Is it true there are pirates?

They could strike again – how will you stop them?!

"I can't reveal all the details of my investigation," explained Inspector Dung. "However, I can tell you that, yes, the crime was committed by pirates. We know this because they left a note at the scene. Using my clever and finely honed detective skills, I have already narrowed these pirates down to two main suspects. All I have to do now is track them down."

Already? thought Stan. Even Inspector SPY-DER couldn't solve a crime that quickly!

Inspector Dung held up a wanted poster.

The crowd oohed.

Captain Ratts and Roachy?! thought Stan, horrified. They weren't burglars – they weren't even pirates!

"Wait a minute!" Stan pushed his way to the front. "What evidence do you have against them, Inspector Dung?"

The Inspector peered over his notebook.

"Ah, Stan Stinky, isn't it? Well, I'm glad you asked. Firstly, we know that the crime was committed by pirates. Captain Ratts dresses like a pirate and his cockroach has a wooden leg. Secondly, we know that the suspects love collecting treasure. Thirdly, those two sneaky crooks have a boat, and everyone knows that pirates have boats. Finally," added Inspector Dung, "they are missing."

There were murmurs of disapproval from the crowd.

Stan wasn't giving up. "But, Inspector Dung, Captain Ratts isn't sneaky or a crook. He's a hero! Isn't he, Mayor?"

The Mayor looked embarrased. "Your Uncle Ratts is my good friend, Stan, but we all know how much he loves an adventure. He's obviously gone too far this time . . . he just can't be trusted." He shook his head sadly and shuffled backwards into the Town Hall, closing the door firmly behind him.

Inspector Dung gave Stan a hard stare. "So Captain Ratts is your uncle, is he? Well, he's also a wanted and dangerous criminal. I hope you will report any sightings to me immediately. Now, if you'll excuse me, I have suspects to catch." He strode off towards the police station.

"Inspector Dung? Inspector Dumb more like!" spluttered Stan once he was out of earshot.

Stan felt a paw on his shoulder. It was Olive.

"Don't worry, Stan," she said gently. "If you say that your uncle isn't the real burglar then I believe you. Let's go back to where The Old Noodle was moored and see if anyone saw what happened to him."

They walked back along the waterfront.

"Hey, look!" said Olive. "This is where Max Weavel's home for Abandoned Pigeons and Other Outcast Pests is meant to be." She pointed to a wonky pipe, then took out the glossy brochure Max Weavels had signed for her in class. "Funny – it doesn't look anything like the picture."

Sitting out at the front, pecking at some crumbs and looking very dirty and forlorn, was a pigeon.

Olive strode over to him. "Hi, I'm Olive," she said, "and this is Stan. We're doing an important investigation to find my stolen guard ant, Stan's uncle and his cockroach friend. Could you answer some questions for us?"

The pigeon looked around as if surprised to be spoken to. "Bob's the name. I suppose I could answer some questions – it's not like I have anything else to do here. . ." He gazed miserably at the pipe behind him.

"But surely you're having a great time living at the home?" asked Olive.

"I would be . . . if I could get in. I knocked on the door but there's no one there," said Bob sadly.

"Perhaps it hasn't opened yet."

"That is strange, isn't it, Stan?" Olive said. Stan nodded. It was very strange indeed.

"Bob, did you see what happened to The Old Noodle? It's usually moored right here."

"Well, I did see something last night," Bob began.

Stan took out his notebook. . .

Witness name: Bob the Pigeon

Should live: At Max Weavel's home for Abandoned Pigeons and Other Outcast Pests (A POOP)

Lives: Currently homeless

Witness account: "It was dark as it was quite late at night, so I couldn't see that much, but I heard a lot of shouting coming from The Old Noodle. I thought that Captain Ratts and Roachy were just practising for one of their adventures — they do that sometimes — but then I heard the engine start and The Old Noodle swerved out of the harbour. It was zigzagging all over the place as it sailed off."

"That doesn't sound right," Stan told Olive. "The Captain and Roachy are excellent sailors!"

Bob yawned. "And they haven't come back," he finished.

Stan rolled up his notebook.

"Well, thanks for your help, Bob. You know, we'll help you find another place to live once we've solved this mystery and got our friends back," he added.

Bob looked pleased. "That would be swell."

Stan and Olive started to walk away.

"Oh – there's one more thing," said Bob. "See that bottle? Someone threw it out of the boat."

He lifted a wing and pointed over the jetty to where a large bottle was floating in a pool of scum.

Chapter 5
A Lot of Bottle

"Left a bit! Right a bit! Left some more!"
Olive was trying to help Stan, who was
leaning over the side of the jetty,
attempting to loop a shoelace
around the neck of
the bottle.

"Got it!" cried Stan, hauling it up.

The bottle was made of green glass and was almost as big as Stan himself. They could just about make out that it contained something.

"A message in a bottle, just like in a book!" Olive was leaping from one foot to another with excitement.

"It must be a very long message," Stan groaned. "It's so heavy!"

Finally he hauled the bottle out and it landed on the jetty. CLINK! POP! The cork flew out.

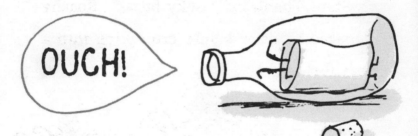

said the bottle.

Stan and Olive stared in astonishment. Did the bottle just talk?

Then to their surprise, a cross-eyed and slightly squished cockroach tumbled out.

"Roachy!?" Stan exclaimed. "Is that you?"

"Stan! Thank my yucky farts!" Roachy managed to utter before crumpling into a heap at their feet.

"Oh dear, he's fainted!" Olive rummaged in the bottom of her bag and found one of Antony's jam sandwiches. It had been there such a long time, it was oozing sticky mould and smelled sickly sweet and rotten. She wafted it under Roachy's antennae.

When Roachy came to, he looked even more dazed than normal.

"Roachy! Why were you in a bottle?!" Stan asked.

"I'm a message," Roachy explained. "From your uncle!"

"Captain Ratts?" gasped Stan. "What happened to him?"

Roachy's face darkened. "KIDNAPPED!"
he cried. "By pirates! Nasty, 'orrible burglar
pirates!"

"Slow down," said Olive, "and
tell us exactly what
happened."

Roachy took a
deep breath. "Me
an' Cap'ain Ratts,
we were minding
our own business
when these 'orrible
pirates appeared.
They stole The Old
Noodle and kidnapped
the Cap'ain.

Luckily, the Cap'ain thought fast and chucked me overboard in that bottle. I heard them say they were heading to the Bananas!"

Oh NO, thought Stan. *Captain Ratts was in serious trouble!*

Just then, he heard a familiar voice and turned round to see Inspector Dung, holding a magnifying glass and examining the place where The Old Noodle had been.

"Quick, Olive!" Stan whispered. "Roachy is a main suspect – we mustn't let Inspector Dung arrest him!"

He grabbed Olive and Roachy and ran down a side pipe. "In here!" he gasped, and dragged them into a darkened shop.

"Phew," whispered Stan.

"Wow!" said Roachy, turning the lights on. "A fancy dress shop!"

"This is Max Weavel's Fancy Dress Shop," said Stan, looking at the sign on the wall.

"Never mind that!" exclaimed Olive. "What's our next move?"

"Well, we know that the pirates are on their way to the Bananas in The Old Noodle," said Stan.

"That doesn't help us much," Olive sighed. "How are we going to get to the Bananas if we don't have a boat?"

"What 'bout the dinghy?" asked Roachy.

"It will take us years to row there in that!" Stan groaned.

"Not any more," grinned Roachy. "Cap'ain Ratts put a motor in it!"

"OK," said Stan, feeling more hopeful. "So we know their location and how to get there. What else do we need for a rescue mission?" He took out his notebook.

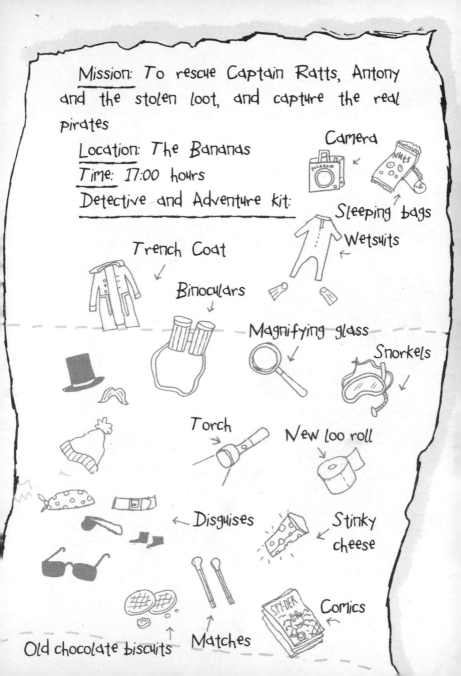

Mission: To rescue Captain Ratts, Antony and the stolen loot, and capture the real pirates

Location: The Bananas

Time: 17:00 hours

Detective and Adventure kit:

Camera

Sleeping bags

Wetsuits

Trench Coat

Binoculars

Magnifying glass

Snorkels

Torch

New loo roll

Disguises

Stinky cheese

Comics

Old chocolate biscuits

Matches

"We're taking disguises?" Olive asked.

"Yes," said Stan. "A real detective always needs a disguise. And luckily, we're in a fancy dress shop!"

Chapter 6
Stakeout in the Bananas

"Are we really going in THAT?"

Olive looked in horror at the dinghy: half a plastic bottle, patched up with Blu-tack.

"It's not my favourite boat either," Stan said, "but at least it has a motor now."

"How does that work?" Olive asked.

"Er . . ." Stan looked a little unsure. "I suppose you just pull this. . ." He pulled the motor cord.

BRRRRROOOOM! The dinghy burst into action.

"WHOA!" Stan grabbed the tiller.

"I THOUGHT WE WERE SUPPOSED TO LEAVE QUIETLY!" Olive shouted over the engine.

"TOO LATE!" Stan shouted back.

The dinghy zoomed out of the harbour and on to the wide River Gunk. Slime-on-the-Sewer and Bob the pigeon quickly disappeared out of sight.

Olive shone the torch ahead while Stan swerved the dinghy this way and that, avoiding the stinky poos that were floating by on all sides.

The journey took most of the night. After a while Stan let Roachy take over, and he and Olive managed to nap for a few hours.

When they awoke, they were almost there. Stan could just make out the shape of the Bananas, an old banana box island piled high with sand, floating in the middle of the River Gunk.

"Let's hide behind that," said Olive, pointing to a half-submerged rusty can of lemonade. Human trash was always finding its way into the sewers.

Roachy turned off the engine, paddled over and dropped the anchor.

Stan took the binoculars out from his Detective-Adventure kit and focused them on the island. Then he snapped some photos and stuck them in his notebook, carefully adding labels.

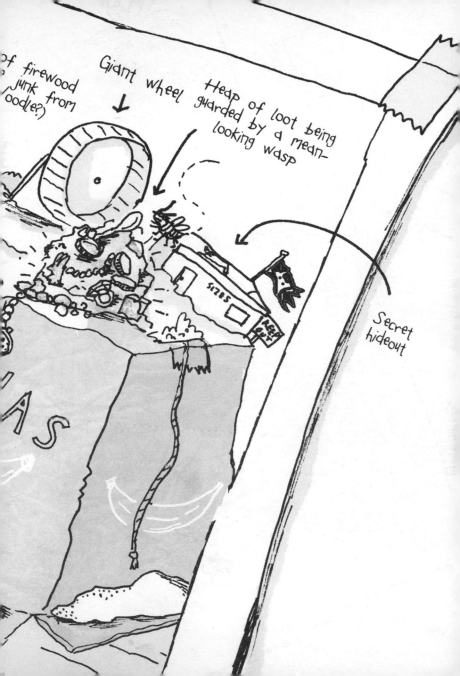

I'm sure I've seen that mean-looking wasp somewhere before, thought Stan.

"What's that massive wheel?" asked Olive.

Roachy took a look.

"Ah, that'll be one of those exercise wheels 'umans put in rat cages when they keep 'em as pets. Supposed to do exercise in them! Haha!"

"Why on earth would the pirates want one of those?" Olive asked.

Hmm, thought Stan.

That WAS curious.

"Look," he hissed. "Here come the pirates!"

Captain Ratts tied up

Antony

"Thank Sewers! Uncle Ratts is all right!!"
Stan said.

"And there's Antony!" Olive couldn't
help squeaking with delight. Antony looked
all right too – in fact, a little bit better than

all right. *Is he fatter than before?* thought Stan. *Someone has obviously been feeding him well.*

Stan turned to Olive and Roachy. "It's time for stage one of the plan," he said. "But we have to wait for nightfall. . . Now, Roachy, where are the chocolate biscuits?"

When nightfall came, Stan, Olive and Roachy snorkled to the shore and silently climbed out on to land. They crept (or rather, squelched) through the sand dunes until they reached a clearing where they spotted the pirates sitting around a campfire.

Quickly they hid behind a palm tree. Stan held up a paw for them to be silent. "I can hear them talking!" he whispered.

He put a loo-roll tube to his ear, straining to hear what they were saying.

"Just tell us where this famous gold tap of yours is!" hissed the pirate who seemed to be in charge. He had an eyepatch and a beard, and looked rather familiar to Stan.

NEVER!

"Never!" shouted Captain Ratts, his defiant cry echoing across the water. "And furthermore," he continued, "you do realize you're the worst pirates I've ever seen on all my travels through the sewers? For one thing, you're far too clean. And what's this obsession with keeping fit in that ridiculous wheel? Most pirates don't care what they look like—"

"ENOUGH!" The pirate leader snapped his paws at the wasp, who was waiting nearby. "Guard him carefully. And if he tells you anything about where the gold tap is, come and get me right away." He laughed an evil laugh, rubbing his paws together.

Ahhh . . . it's goooood to be baaaaad!

Hmm, thought Stan. That sounded VERY familiar . . . "Right," he whispered to Olive and Roachy, "time for stage two of the plan. Roachy, you go back to the dinghy and keep watch. Olive and I will camp here until morning. Then . . ." he said, putting on a big belt and an eyepatch and handing Olive a headscarf and pair of boots, "we're going undercover . . . as PIRATE ADVISORS!"

Chapter 7
Undercover Pirates

At first light, Stan and Olive left their sandy hiding place in full disguise.

They'd barely taken two steps when a voice said, "Oi! Zzzz! What do we have here?"

It was the wasp.

"You need to BUZZZZZZZ OFF!" The wasp frowned. "Thizzz izzz no place for little ratzzz." He flew right up to Stan's face, buzzing angrily.

"Let me handle this," Olive whispered. "Excuse me, Mr . . . ?"

The wasp turned towards her. "Stinger. Not that it'zzzz any of your businesszzz."

Olive continued, "Mr Stinger, we are well known and IMPORTANT pirate advisors." She handed the wasp a handmade business card. "I, myself, have many weeks' experience in training pirate pets and finding and maintaining valuable treasure hoards. My associate here is an expert in walking-the-plank technique and pirate clothing and accessories. "

We are PiRATe Advisors!

Happy to HELP

- Training pirate pets
- Finding TREASURE hoards
- Walking plank techniques
- Clothing and Accessory advice

Stan smiled. Olive was good at this!

"We were informed that new pirates were in the area, and having seen you . . . well, we thought you might be in need of our services."

Stinger glared at them suspiciously. "What makezz you think we need your help?"

"Oh!" Olive smiled. "Everyone needs help sometimes."

The wasp hesitated and Stan said quickly, "Look, Mr Stinger, we know your pirate friends will be very annoyed if you send us away without introducing us to them first. Surely they'd like to decide for themselves."

Stinger thought about this and rolled his eyes. "Zzzstay RIGHT HERE," he hissed and flew off.

Stan and Olive sighed in relief, but before they could exchange a word, Stinger was back.

"The bosszzz wantzzz to meet you. But I've told him, I don't truszzzt you one bit," he buzzed haughtily. "Follow me."

It was gloomy inside the pirates' hideout and as Stan's eyes adjusted to the light he saw the place was piled high with bottle tops. In one corner, some of the pirates were playing a game of tiddlywinks with them.

"Those bottle tops are my dad's!" Olive whispered crossly under her breath.

"Ah, so here are our little intruders." The pirate leader was lounging in a hammock and munching through a bottle top full of dried peas. *Dried peas again*! thought Stan.

"I am Captain Weavelbeard, the most feared pirate in all the Seven Sewers." The pirate twirled his moustache, scratched his nose and readjusted his eyepatch, which looked very new. "I've been told you are pirate advisors." He raised an eyebrow.

"We most certainly are. I am Olive the

Awesome and this is Putrid-Pants Stan, my associate," Olive said smoothly. Stan frowned. Those were not the names they'd agreed on.

She continued. "And we are more than happy to offer you our services in pet training, latest piratical fashion and, of course, obtaining and maintaining stolen loot."

Captain Weavelbeard sat up. "Stolen loot, eh?" A greedy smile spread across his face. "Interesting. . ."

We could do with some extra paws,

"We could do with some extra paws," said the angry pirate, one of the group playing tiddlywinks. She flicked another bottle top across the room and Olive winced.

"Our next raid is the BIG one," said the short pirate.

"We can always feed them to the sewer sharks if they turn out to be rubbish," added the tall one.

"Tiver me shimbers," said the one-eared pirate.

Stan gulped, but then remembered there weren't sharks in the sewer and the pirate must be bluffing.

"Fine!" said Captain Weavelbeard. "You can stay on a trial basis. But if you mess up . . ."

he leaned in menacingly, and Stan caught a whiff of some horribly familiar aftershave.

You don't have to worry about that,

Stan said quickly. "We're the best."

Weavelbeard looked pleased. "Of course, our plan is so top secret, we can't possibly tell you where our next raid is going to take place. But I can tell you it's tomorrow so there is lots of toilsome work to be done!" He paused, then chuckled. "It's gooood to be baaaad!"

Stan and Olive glanced at each other. They had successfully infiltrated the pirates . . . but how were they supposed to stop them? They didn't even know where Captain Weavelbeard was planning to raid next.

They needed to talk to Captain Ratts.

Stan and Olive looked down at a snoozing Captain Ratts. They had offered to interrogate the prisoner to try and find out where the gold tap was hidden, and Weavelbeard had eagerly agreed. But Stinger was hovering suspiciously, so they had to be careful.

"Wake up, you scurvy rodent!" Stan said.

The captain snored away.

Stan prodded his uncle. "WAKE UP! Arr, I'm Putrid-Pants Stan and I'm here to interrogate you!"

"What? What . . . !?" The Captain rubbed his bleary eyes and couldn't hide his confusion at seeing his favourite nephew standing in front of him in fancy dress.

"YIP! YIP! YIP!"

Antony had woken up too, and was leaping all over Olive, licking her face in delight.

"Er, I have a way with pets," she explained to Stinger.

The wasp gave her a strange look, but then, to their relief, they heard Captain Weavelbeard calling, "Stinger! Get over here and fetch me some sparkling mineral water . . . I mean, grog."

Stinger gave them one last suspicious look and buzzed off.

"Stan! What the devil is going on?" Captain Ratts whispered. "Where's Roachy?

In hushed tones Stan explained everything that had happened back in Slime-on-the-Sewer, how Ratts and Roachy were the main suspects for the robberies, and how Stan and Olive had come to the Bananas in disguise to try and rescue them.

"But now we've found out the pirates are

planning a big raid tomorrow and we don't know how to stop them. We're trapped on the island and we have no way of getting word to Inspector Dung or the Mayor," he finished.

"Well, you've certainly been busy!" said Ratts cheerfully. "I'm sure you two will think of something. And don't forget Roachy – he's never let me down yet." He smiled reassuringly at Stan and pushed his uneaten breakfast of dried peas towards Antony, who gulped them down.

Stan opened his mouth to say more but just then Stinger flew back over.

"Buzzz! Have you found out any useful information yet?"

Stan put on his piratey voice again. "This is your LAST CHANCE, Captain Ratts. Tell me where that gold tap is . . . or . . . or else!"

"Oooh!" Captain Ratts pretended to be scared. "I'll never tell!" Then, "Good job, Stan," he whispered under his breath.

Chapter 8
A Secret Scroll

Captain Weavelbeard kept Stan and Olive busy for the rest of the day. Olive was put to work training Antony to sniff for gold. Stan showed the pirates swashbuckling moves with bananas.

When the pirates stopped for some lunch (more dried peas), Stan wrote down clues in his notebook.

LATEST CLUES

The pirates are rubbish at being pirates

They are wearing clean clothes - some still have labels on!

To Hire

Don't have cutlasses

Having to use bananas!

They keep eating dried peas

The pirate leader's aftershave is awful. He wears lots of it, and it smells familiar

EAU de LOO

Catchphrase of Pirate leader Weavelbeard

It's goooood to be baaad!

"Putrid-Pants Stan, get over here." It was Captain Weavelbeard.

Stan gulped. Had he figured them out? Was it time to make a run for it?

"Do you think I should wear these for the raid tomorrow?" Weavelbeard pointed to his pair of brand-new trousers.

Stan couldn't help but snigger. "Aren't they a bit too . . . well-ironed for a pirate? In fact if you don't mind me saying so, you look far too smart."

"I'm the sort of pirate who likes things shipshape," Weavelbeard huffed. "However, I take your point."

Stan spent the whole evening turning a fancy jacket into a ragged pirate waistcoat and cutting zigzags into Weavelbeard's pirate trousers. He was just hanging them up again when he noticed something in the back pocket.

A scroll.

He glanced around the hideout. Olive and the pirates were already fast asleep in their hammocks, although he could make out the shape of Stinger buzzing around outside.

Stan carefully removed the scroll from the pocket and unrolled it.

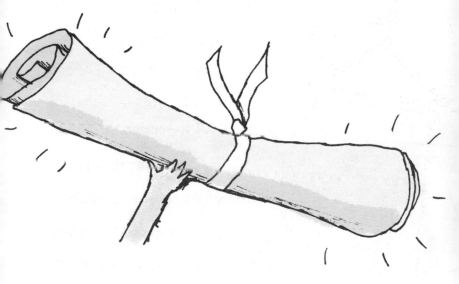

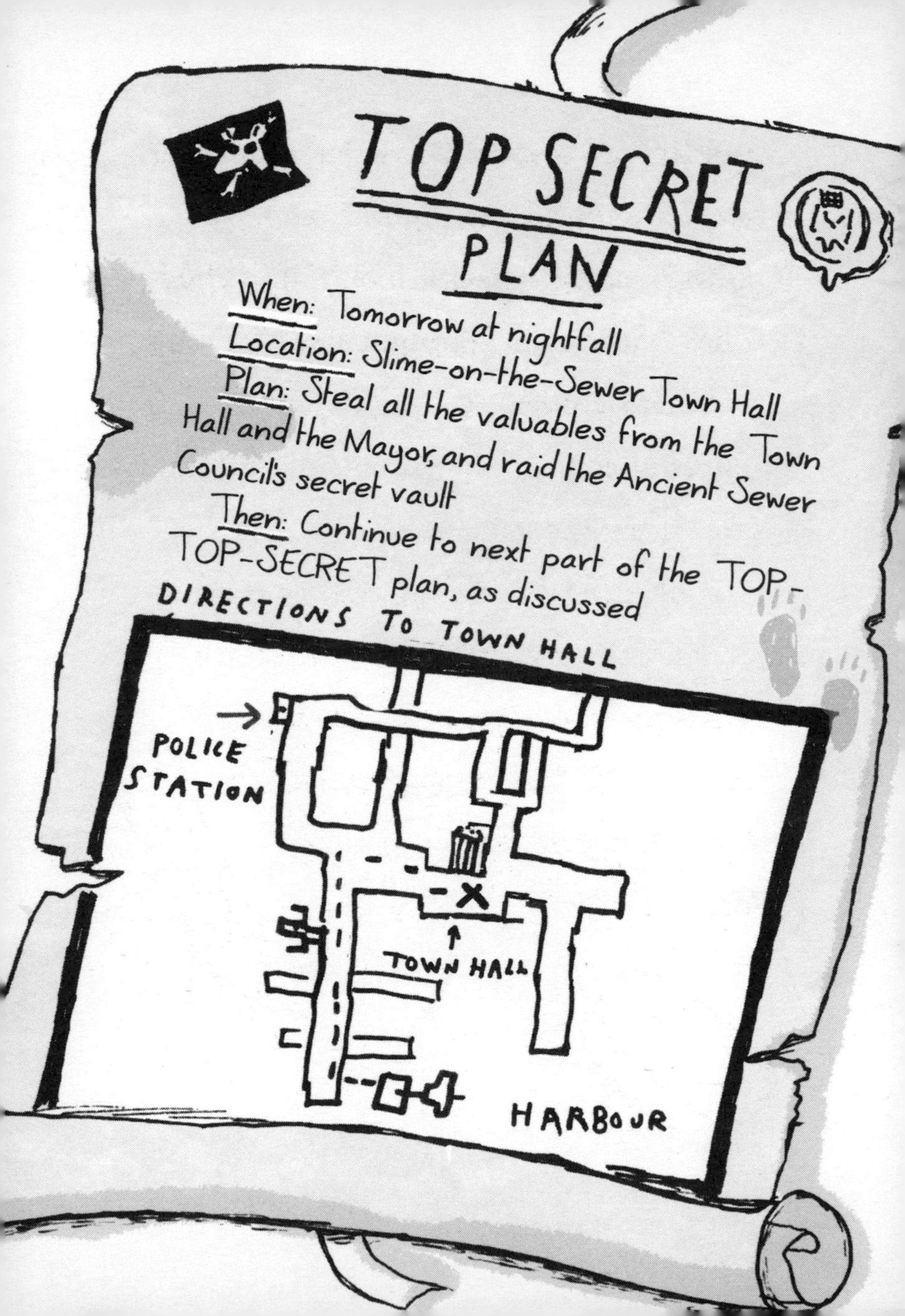

TOP SECRET
PLAN

When: Tomorrow at nightfall

Location: Slime-on-the-Sewer Town Hall

Plan: Steal all the valuables from the Town Hall and the Mayor, and raid the Ancient Sewer Council's secret vault

Then: Continue to next part of the TOP-SECRET plan, as discussed

DIRECTIONS TO TOWN HALL

POLICE STATION

TOWN HALL

HARBOUR

Stan tiptoed over to Olive. He shook her awake and showed her what he'd found.

"Oh no!" she whispered, looking horrified. "We have no way of letting Inspector Dung know what's going on!"

Stan studied the map with his magnifying glass. "I have an idea," he said.

He picked up his eraser and rubbed out the X. Then he put an X in another place.

"What are you doing?" asked Olive.

Stan smiled. "Just changing the location of the raid . . . to the police station."

By nightfall the next day, the pirates were ready to set off on their raid.

"Stinger, you stay here and guard our prisoners and the treasure," ordered Weavelbeard. "The rest of you, get ready to, er, what's the phrase . . . cast off! Yo ho ho!"

So Uncle Ratts isn't coming with us, thought Stan. That meant he and Olive would be facing the pirates alone.

"Wait a minute!" Olive ran and scooped up Antony. "I have trained this ant to, er . . . sniff out gold. He'll be very useful!"

"Very well then," said Captain Weavelbeard. "Now, off we go."

sang the pirates, and they joked and boasted about how rich they were going to be.

Stan's heart dropped as he watched Captain Ratts and the Bananas fade from view. He craned his neck to see if he could spot Roachy, the dinghy and the rusty lemonade can, but they had vanished. There was no time to warn Roachy anyway. They were on their way.

Chapter 9
A Plan Destroyed

The evening of the raid was a dreary
one. Warm, smelly mists rolled off the
River Gunk and the darkness seemed
to swallow them whole. The only light
in the pipes came from a flickering
candle that was stuck to the helm
of The Old Noodle.

After long hours of bumpy sailing, finally The Old Noodle was bobbing up and down just outside the harbour of Slime-on-the-Sewer. The lights from the pipe homes shone out across the water. Stan wished he could shout loud enough to warn everyone. But even Olive wasn't loud enough for that!

The pirates were crammed into the cabin having a secret meeting. Stan and Olive had been told to keep watch.

Stan peered in through the porthole. They were looking at the map of Slime-on-the-Sewer by torchlight. Stan hoped that they hadn't noticed the changes he'd made to the map.

"Arr, I can't wait!" The tall pirate was rubbing his paws with glee.

"Nor me!" said the short one.

"It's going to be brrrrillliant!" agreed the angry pirate.

"Tiver me shimbers!" said the rat with one ear.

"I think they've fallen for it!" Stan gave a thumbs up to Olive. He crept closer so that he could hear what they were saying.

Weavelbeard gave his crew a huge evil grin. "The best part, of course, is what happens after the raid."

Stan's ears pricked up.

"Once we're back on the Bananas, we'll collect the rest of our treasure and leave a forged note that frames Captain Ratts for all our crimes!" He laughed cruelly. "That STUPID Inspector Dung already thinks the first raid was done by him, so it should be easy." He waved the note in the air.

"Now, let's go over the route," he continued. "So it's left out of the harbour, then right down Manky Street, up Crusty Pipe Lane and then . . . hang on a second! This isn't where the Town Hall is! Someone's changed the map!"

Oh NO! Captain Weavelbeard had noticed!

"What are we going to do!" whispered Stan to Olive. "He'll soon figure out that it was me. And now there's no way of warning Inspector Dung!"

Olive thought quickly. "I've got it. We CAN send a warning to the Inspector and the Mayor. We just need a postal fly!"

Her idea was their only hope and they didn't have a second to lose. Stan knew that to attract flies you needed something really smelly. "I've got it!" he cried. "The cheese from my Detective-Adventure kit!"

Holding their noses, Stan and Olive ran to the side of the boat. They tied the oozing Gorgonzola to the end of a mop and Olive dangled it over the edge, so it could waft in the breeze.

Stan hastily scribbled a note:

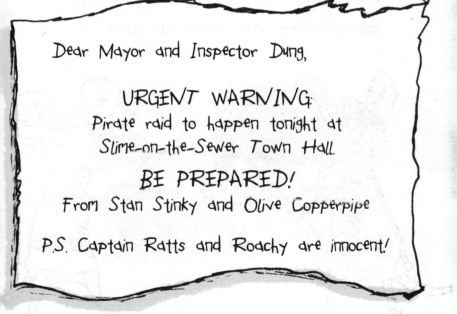

Dear Mayor and Inspector Dung,

URGENT WARNING:
Pirate raid to happen tonight at Slime-on-the-Sewer Town Hall.

BE PREPARED!
From Stan Stinky and Olive Copperpipe

P.S. Captain Ratts and Roachy are innocent!

He sealed the letter with a smear of Gorgonzola and sure enough, they soon heard the drone of beating wings and saw their cheese had drawn quite a bit of interest.

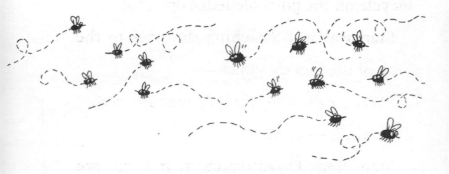

There were flies swarming everywhere. Among them Stan spotted a fly with a little red bicycle.

"Postal delivery, please!" Stan waved the letter to attract its attention. The postal fly looked rather confused to be posting anything so late, but he landed his small bicycle on the porthole ledge opening.

Stan was just attaching the note to the back of the bicycle when—

"Well, well, well, what do we have here?" a booming voice said.

Stan and Olive spun round to see Weavelbeard towering over them, a nasty smile on his face. "Sending some post, are we? I don't suppose you'll mind if I have a read?"

He picked up the postal fly and plucked the message from his bicycle.

"Just as I thought! Traitors! Did you actually think I wouldn't notice my map had been tampered with? Ha! It will take more than two snivelling little ratlings to trick Captain Weavelbeard."

Stan and Olive were suddenly surrounded by pirates on all sides. In seconds their paws had been tied behind their backs.

"I should have listened to Stinger. You ARE good-for-nothing, scheming little maggots!" Weavelbeard raged. "Now, let me think of a really terrible pirate punishment . . ." He paused. "Er, a really terrible pirate punishment, like, er . . . er. . ."

"Please don't make us WALK THE PLANK!" Olive sobbed.

"That's it! Walking the plank it is! After all, you did claim you were experts on it," Weavelbeard cackled wickedly. "Let's get moving – I can't wait to get out of this RIDICULOUS COSTUME!"

"I knew it!" Stan cried. "I KNEW you weren't real pirates. In fact, I think I know exactly who you all are!"

"Well, it's too late now, squirt!" said Weavelbeard with an evil sneer, and he pushed Stan and Olive on to the plank. "Why don't you tell it to the poos in the River Gunk!"

"Help! Someone! Help!" cried Olive as the plank creaked unsteadily beneath their paws. She caught sight of Antony,

munching on the piece of mouldy
Gorgonzola.

But it was too late. The plank broke and
Stan and Olive tumbled overboard!

Stan and Olive were in the water. It was freezing cold and because their front paws were tied, they could only move their legs and tails to keep themselves afloat.

"We . . . need . . . to . . . try . . . and swim," Olive gasped.

But it was no use – they could only just keep their heads above water.

"HELP!" yelled Stan. "HEEELLP!" But The Old Noodle sped away, with the pirates cackling in glee.

"We're going to SINK," cried Olive.

Just then – SWOOSH! – a
large winged creature
zoomed over their
heads. It was Bob the
Pigeon!

With a few snaps of his beak, Bob freed
them and scooped them
on to his back. Stan and
Olive clung to his
feathers as he flew
them high into the
air to safety.

"Bob! You saved us! How did you know where we were?"

"I was asleep, having a dream about a tasty pasty . . . haven't eaten one of those in years," Bob sighed. "Anyway, then I heard squeaking and I thought I should probably investigate."

"Thank you!" Stan said. "But we need to hurry. There's going to be a raid tonight at the Town Hall. We have to alert Slime-on-the-Sewer! Can you take us?"

"Well, I guess I can. Nothing better to do . . ." Bob said. He soared round in a circle and flew over Slime-on-the-Sewer, aiming for the Town-Hall roof.

"Get ready to land!" he called, as they plummeted downwards.

Olive yelled.

"We're going to—"
THUMP!

"Need to practise my landings," said Bob sheepishly. "I don't think I'll be flying again for a while."

"No worries, Bob," Stan said, feeling a little dizzy.

He peered over the edge of the roof and, to his horror, saw Weavelbeard hurrying out of the big double doors, carrying a large, gold-framed painting and a sack of loot.

He looked around frantically and spotted two loudspeakers that the Mayor used to make announcements.

His voice echoed over the pipe tops and across the town, rattling the windows.

"Whoa! That was loud!" Olive had her paws over her ears.

They watched as light after light came on in the town. Rats and bugs stuck their heads out of windows and doors, and stumbled outside in their pyjamas. The pirates had heard Stan too, and he could see them running towards the harbour.

Luckily Inspector
Dung was in hot
pursuit.

"Where's the Mayor?"
said Olive. "The pirates
must have got him!"

Stan, Olive and Bob hurried into the
Town Hall. When they reached the top of
the staircase they heard a low groaning noise
coming from the Mayor's bedroom.

"He must be hurt,"
gasped
Stan.

All three of them banged hard
on his door.

"Mayor, it's Stan and Olive! We've come to save you!"

There was a snuffling noise and a loud thump.

"The pirates must have tied him up!" cried Olive. "Let's break the door down. One, two—"

Just then the door creaked open and the Mayor appeared, wearing a dressing gown and fluffy slippers, and looking very grumpy.

"What in the sewer is going on?" he humphed. "Why have you woken me up?"

Stan and Olive couldn't believe it. The mayor had slept through everything!

"You've been raided by PIRATES!" Olive yelled.

"Nonsense!" the Mayor said. "I would have noticed if pirates had raided my own home. . ."

He looked around and then noticed in horror the empty walls where his prized art collection had been.

"Quick, follow us!" Stan cried.

Stan, Olive, Bob and the Mayor dashed towards the harbour, the Mayor puffing and panting with the effort.

They arrived just as The Old Noodle was sailing off. Half the town was there, watching helplessly.

Inspector Dung was leaping furiously from leg to leg. "GNNNNNNRRR!"

"What happened?" cried Stan.

"Those scurvy pirates untied all the other boats in the harbour, so we couldn't go after them!"

"They can't be getting away!" Stan said to Olive. "And they've still got Antony!"

Olive groaned. "We've failed."

The Mayor stared in dismay at the disappearing boat, floating away with his precious things.

Stan put his head in his paws. After all their successful detecting and clever plans, Captain Weavelbeard had got away with his crime.

"Wait a minute. . ." Olive was peering at the dark horizon. "Something is coming."

Stan looked up. At first he couldn't see anything but then he realized that Olive was right. A dark shape was moving over the water towards them. He could see a flickering light bobbing up and down. Could it be. . . ?

"It's CAPTAIN RATTS!" yelled Stan as the dinghy came into view, gaining fast on The Old Noodle. Roachy was with him, holding a burning match to light the way. Stan also spotted Stinger, looking miserable in a cage.

The crowd on the harbour oohed and aahed as Captain Ratts grabbed the Old Noodle's plunger...

heaved it down...
and fastened it to the bottom of the sewer pipe.

CREAK!
SCHLURP!

The pirates cursed and stamped their feet and tried to pull themselves free, but it was too late – they were well and truly STUCK!

"Hurrah!" Olive and Stan clapped and everyone else joined in. Captain Ratts had saved the day in typical swashbuckling fashion.

Chapter 11
Stan's Big Moment

Slime-on-the-Sewer was bustling with excitement in the morning light. All the residents of the town were awake and gathering on the harbour. Everyone wanted to see the infamous pirates.

Inspector Dung had arrested the whole crew and Stinger had been handed over, buzzing with insults. The Inspector apologized to Captain Ratts – he was pretty embarrassed that he'd thought Ratts and Roachy were the main suspects – but Captain Ratts wasn't worried. He was too busy signing autographs.

Inspector Dung lined up the pirates ready to go to the police station. "You pirates are under arrest," he said importantly. "For burglary and looting."

"WAIT A MINUTE!" cried the Mayor. "There should be six pirates. I can only see five."

Everyone looked. It was true – there were just five pirates now, including Stinger. Captain Weavelbeard was missing.

"Sound the alarm!" Inspector Dung yelled. "We have an ESCAPED PRISONER! Nobody move!"

"An escaped prisoner, already?" A concerned voice came from behind Stan. It was Max Weavels, looking as dapper as ever. "How shocking, Inspector Dung! I leave the sewer for a few days to attend a charity event and disaster strikes."

Inspector Dung turned crimson. "I can assure you, Mr Weavels, he won't have gone far." He scanned the crowd desperately.

"He hasn't!" Stan piped up, turning to face Max Weavels. "In fact, he's standing right here!"

The crowd gasped.

"What do you mean, Stan?" cried Inspector Dung.

"Yes, what DO you mean?" asked Max Weavels.

"I mean that Max Weavels and Captain Weavelbeard are one and the same!"

"Stan Stinky!" Inspector Dung exclaimed. "Max Weavels is a respected member of our community. Mr Weavels, I'm so sorry – Stan, I think you should apologize to Mr Weavels."

"Don't worry, Inspector," Max laughed. "This little rat just has a very active imagination."

"Oh, is that so? Then how come this crew are not real pirates? How come they look exactly like the so-called reformed criminals you employed in your home for Abandoned Pigeons and Other Outcast Pests?" cried Stan. He marched along the line-up, tugging at the pirates' moustaches and pulling off their eyepatches and scarves.

"You see," said Stan, holding up the A POOP brochure.

The crowd gasped again.

"Well, I never!" cried the Mayor. "How on earth did you figure it out, Stan?"

"I first noticed something was up when Max Weavels came to our school. He seemed VERY interested in Olive's dad's bottle top collection. He made sure that Inspector Dung was away on holiday by sending him there himself, and then planned the first raid in Brownwater with his fake pirate crew."

"The first clue." Olive held up the envelope containing the dried pea they'd found. "This pea was discovered at the scene of the burglary. It's food that humans feed rats in the rat prison, Rat-a-Traz, which is where Max got a taste for them."

"Max claimed to be building a home for pigeons and other pests," continued Stan. "But when we interviewed Bob, he revealed that the home wasn't even open."

"And it was obvious they weren't real pirates," piped up Captain Ratts. "For one thing, they didn't know how to steer the boat. For another thing, they kept exercising in that giant wheel. And their clothes were way too clean."

"That's because their outfits came from Max's fancy dress shop," explained Stan. "But the real clincher was Max himself – even when he was disguised as a pirate he couldn't stop wearing his famous aftershave. I believe his favourite Eau de Loo Cleaner scent is Pine Fresh."

Stan handed Inspector Dung his detective notebook. "It's all in here."

"I – I don't know what to say," said Inspector Dung.

"I see," the Mayor said, turning to Max. "It looks like your time as a criminal really is over once and for all, Max Weavels."

Max gave Stan a bitter little smile. "Well, well, well," he said. "So you figured it out. Unfortunate. My plans were shaping up so nicely. After I stole the loot, I was going to turn the home for Abandoned Pigeons and Other Outcast Pests into a luxury mansion. I'd have been right under your noses, enjoying your treasure every day, and you wouldn't have known." He sighed. "Shame it won't work out. Then again, I have always wanted to travel. . ."

Fast as lightning, Max Weavels turned and ran, straight out on a jetty and dived into the water.

"He's getting away! Someone stop him!" boomed the Mayor.

"It's too late!" gasped Stan. But then—

"ANTONY!" Olive cried. "I KNEW you had it in you!"

Stan had to admit, Antony was a star. It seemed all his eating had paid off – he had been getting big and strong. "He makes a much better guard ant now," Stan told Olive, as Inspector Dung led the spluttering Max Weavels away. "After all, he has just captured the sewer's most wanted criminal!"

Chapter 12
Treasure Returned

Stan, Olive, Antony, Captain Ratts and Roachy were on their way to Brownwater. The Old Noodle (pirate flag removed) was loaded with the boxes of treasure.

They'd already helped the Mayor take the goods back to the Town Hall and now Captain Ratts had been entrusted with the task of returning the rest of the valuables to their owners.

Stan's uncle certainly seemed to be enjoying the task.

"Now, remember, everyone needs to take the right boxes back to the right places. Stan, you're taking that load of boxes to the Museum of Shiny Things Accidentally Washed Down Human Plugholes and Roachy, you're taking the teaspoon and these garden ornaments back. . . And I'm donating my gold tap to the home for A POOP so that Bob will finally have somewhere to live."

"That's amazing, Captain Ratts! And I'll take my dad's bottle tops and Antony back home," Olive

said. "He's never going to believe how well trained and strong Antony is now."

Captain Ratts sighed and scratched the top of Antony's head. "I'll miss the little chap's company," he admitted.

"I think he'll miss your scraps," Olive laughed. "By the way, how DID you manage to escape and capture Stinger?"

"Oh, it was complicated. . ." The Captain

waved his paws around vaguely. "A team effort, I'd call it."

"*I* captured Stinger," Roachy boasted. "I had been hiding behind an old lemonade can. I thought to meself, wasps like them fizzy drinks, so I rowed closer to the island dragging the can and let's just say, Stinger found 'imself in a sticky situation! Then I freed Cap'ain Ratts. . ."

"And everything else was my idea," said Ratts quickly.

"Good thinking . . . both of you!" Stan said. "Now, let's get these prized possessions back to their rightful owners."

After they'd finally dropped off all the valuables, Stan decided it was time to go home. It had been a great detective adventure, but now he was tired.

"Thank you, Olive," said Stan. "You made an excellent detective."

For once, Olive was speechless.

Stan's mum was relieved when he finally got home. "I just heard the news," she said. "And I thought Max Weavels seemed like such a nice rat. . . But your adventure was very dangerous, Stan! You could have been hurt!"

Stan hung his head.

His mum's stern look turned to a smile. "I'm very proud of you." Then she added, "School tomorrow. It'll feel strange after

all the excitement, won't it?"

School! Stan suddenly realized he still had his Class Talk to do.

Stan needn't have worried. His talk was a huge success. The class were hanging on his every word as he told them all about his detective adventure – when he'd first suspected Max Weavels, how he and Olive had disguised themselves as pirate advisors, and what it was like to walk a plank. Even Mrs Scratchy was impressed. She gave him a gold sticker for his efforts.

When Stan got home, a letter was waiting for him on the mat. *From Captain Ratts*, thought Stan. *But I only saw him yesterday!*

HOME FOR ABANDONED PIGEONS AND OTHER OUTCAST PESTS

Dear Stan,

I've had an amazing idea!
I've been talking to Bob and he says there are lots of needy pigeons and other homeless animals above ground who might want to come and live in the home for Abandoned Pigeons and Other Outcast Pests. What do you think about going to rescue our feathery and furry relations and bringing them back to the sewers? It would mean a potentially dangerous trip to some human-populated places, but I could certainly do with your help – unless you're tired of adventure now?

Yours adventurously,

Captain Ratts

Stan thought about it. On the one hand, his comic book had just arrived, with a new INSPECTOR SPY-DER cartoon inside – and did he really need any more excitement after the last few days? A trip above ground to the perilous human world would be full of hazards. He should just curl up with his magazine and leave the adventuring to his uncle.

On the other hand, he DID have a new loo-roll notebook to fill. . .

THE END

Acknowledgements

Thanks to editorial cap'n's o' words Genevieve Herr and Lena McCauley, design buccaneers Alison Padley and Simon Letchford with the brand new baby Robin. Once again, a big appreciative grin to the swashbuckling Penny Holroyde. And hugs all round for my family and friends, especially Joce and Mum for looking after my squeaky human so I could write this and draw all the pictures without spilt milk splashes and crayon scribbles.

Not forgetting all my readers, especially those at Newnham St Peter's Primary School, West Hill Primary Wandsworth, Horsley Primary School and Rodborough Community Primary School in Stroud and Eagle House School, Berkshire. You are all wonderful!

WHAT'S YOUR

PiRATe

NAME?

Don't turn
the page yet!
(NO SNEAK-PEEKING)

**FIRST YOU'LL NEED TO KNOW THE
MONTH YOU WERE BORN**

**THEN CHOOSE A LUCKY NUMBER FROM
ONE to TWELVE**

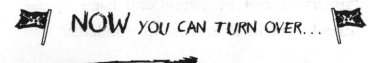

NOW YOU CAN TURN OVER...

OOOH ARRR, you lucky rodent, here's your new piRATe Name!

BIRTH MONTH	Your FIRST NAME
January	Cap'n Manky-Mouse
February	Shiver Me Timbers Slimy
March	Jolly Old Mouldy
April	Grimy Sea-Dog
May	Swashbuckling Scrawny
June	Grungy o' Fish-Head
July	Long-John Yucky
August	Barnacle o'Crusty
September	Cap'n Bones Musty
October	Blistering Buccaneer
November	Pongy Plank-Walker
December	Squid-Breath Scratchy

TREASURE BURYING IN PROGRESS

CHOSEN NO:	Your SECOND NAME
1.	Vermin-Legs
2.	Flea-Beard
3.	Wild-Whiskers
4.	Loo-Raider
5.	Two-Tails
6.	Scab-Nose
7.	Sewer-Bottom
8.	Yellow-Teeth
9.	Bog-Brush-Breath
10.	McStink
11.	Slug-Scarer
12.	Cheese-Cruncher

YOU CAN EVEN MAKE YOURSELF A NAME BADGE!

HELLO, I'm

The most feared PiRATE in the SEVEN SEWERS